I AM

A TREASURE

SEEKER

I AM

A TREASURE

SEEKER

By Paula Range

Illustrated by Paula Range

Cover picture credit to:

Canva.com

ISBN 13: 9781696093521

This book is dedicated to:

My sweet friend, *down the road.* Please
don't believe those hurtful words thrown
your way. You are a treasure. Your smile
is infectious. You are a precious jewel and
loved by many.

Thank you to all who took time to read I AM A TREASURE SEEKER ahead of time. I am thankful for all your help, thoughts, and insights...

Meagan, Izzy, and Aubrey

Makayla

Natalie

Krista

PROLOGUE

Visions. What in the world was happening to me? Falling out of a treehouse, I had hit my head on a rock. Sadly, it had been on a Friday after school with my "friends", so I had all weekend to rest. So, what did that mean? It meant that I didn't get to skip any school. Bummer.

Ever since my fall, I had been seeing visions into people's lives. Not just anyone, but people who'd been bullied by me or others. Am I a bully? Well, hopefully not anymore. But *was* I a bully? To answer truthfully, YES, I WAS A BULLY.

When I started school, my friends were the cool kids. But as the visions began, I slowly saw who I was and who the other kids I had been hurting were. My choice of friends slowly changed. I said "choice" of friends because I realized I had a choice. To step away from bullying others or continue the road I was on.

I chose to step away. May I say, that was the best choice I've ever made. I did not say the easiest, but the best for me.

So, come join me, read on and see where my next visions will take me.

CHAPTER 1

Wow, was I tired. We had just worked all day on a sale at school. It had started as just a school project. The next thing my friend Becky and I knew, it turned into the real thing. Resting in my chair, I had been thinking about all that had taken place these past few hours.

My old friends, Holly, Amy, and Tiffany came and crashed our sale. Well, *tried* to crash our sale. Did they succeed? Almost, but we chose not to let it ruin our day. I mean putting garlic powder on the brownies for sale and dumping hot sauce into the punch was not cool. But we dumped those out and made new punch and put new brownies out and kept going. Raising over two thousand dollars to help other kids in our school with food and school supplies was so worth it. With the sale over, I just wanted to rest my feet for a few minutes.

As I looked around, I saw Mr. Williams, our very *old* janitor. All the kids, me included, had always called him One-Eyed Scar Face. He had a patch over one eye and a huge scar that ran down the same side of his face. Everyone, I mean *everyone,* had always been so scared of him.

I sat there and watched as he started to slowly shuffle from table to table. I watched as he dropped his cleaning rag onto the floor. Now, my old self would have sat there and watched him try to pick it up. But before he could lean down to retrieve it, I jumped out of my seat and called out, "I got it for you, Mr. Williams." I rushed over to help the old, frail, grey-haired man.

Grabbing the rag off the floor, I straightened up and reached out to hand it back to him.

"Thanks so much," he whispered faintly, giving me a strained half-smile. His one eye connected with my eyes and I started to see stars...

There were two kids playing basketball outside.

"Hey, George, shoot!"

"I will!" As George Williams shot the ball, it hit the backboard and bounced into the neighbor's yard.

Both boys froze.

"You go get it, George. You're the one who shot the ball."

"I know, but the stupid big dog is over there. Look, he's sitting there making that low growling noise at us!"

"That's why you need to go."

George looked at his friend and rolled his eyes. "Great friend you are."

"Hey, I just want to live! That dog is mean." After a moment of thinking his friend added, "I know, I'll try to distract him, so he doesn't see you go into their yard. Hey, doggie, doggie. Hey, look at this."

As George's friend tried to get the dog to look the other way, George made a run for it.

He got to the ball, picked it up and turned around to get back into his own yard. He started running, but the dog heard him, saw the movement, and charged.

"Look out, George!"

Within seconds, George found himself on the ground and felt pain.

"Help! Help!"

I could hear George yell, "Oh, my eye! Oh, my face!"

I felt a tug on my hand. Mr. Williams was trying to take the rag I had been holding out to him. During the vision, I must have clung to the rag so tightly he couldn't get it back. Opening my hand so he could grab it, I just stared at him.

He must have seen my confusion because he cleared his throat, "Um, thank you, dear. That was very kind of you. These tired bones of mine have a hard time bending all the way down to pick things up off the floor."

Shaking my head to clear it of the vision, I answered. "Oh, you're welcome, Mr. Williams." I studied his face, realizing that a dog had been the one to put those scars on his face. After a pause, I added, "Have a nice day, and thanks for helping us clean up."

Now it was his turn to be staring at me, because no one ever talked to him. And if they did, let me just say it wasn't something nice.

CHAPTER 2

As soon as we finished cleaning up the cafeteria, I found my mom, and asked if we could go home. I usually keep my visions to myself, but I really wanted to talk to someone about this one. Since my sister Grace was the only one I had told about my visions, she was who I needed to talk to.

"Grace," I whispered as we entered the house. "Meet me up in my room as soon as you can."

Looking at me strangely, she leaned my way and whispered back, "Okay, but why are we whispering?"

Ugh. Rolling my eyes, I tried to shake my head towards my mom. "I just have to talk to you about something, okay?"

"Oh, like secretive. This is so fun!" She looked around to make sure no one heard us and rubbed her hands together. "Okay, sis, I'll meet you there shortly." She walked off, looking both ways. I realized she was trying to sneak around like a detective.

Smiling, I shook my head. My sister was such a goofball. She could make me laugh even if I was in a bad mood. Being only a year and a half younger than myself, Grace had a totally different personality than me. She was goofy and happy, while I was the more serious one.

Once I entered my room, I threw my coat on the floor and plopped on my bed. As I lay there, I couldn't help but think about the vision of Mr. Williams.

My thoughts were interrupted when my sister entered the room, and I couldn't help but laugh. "Oh my gosh! What in the world are you doing?"

She was wearing my dad's dress coat, and his sunglasses were covering her eyes. She had a hat on her head and my grandma's magnifying glass in her hand, that she used for word search puzzles.

"I'm here to help!" She walked mysteriously over and held out her hand. "Detective Gray at your service."

"Detective who?"

"Gray. I mean come on Cat, Detective Grace wouldn't sound too mysterious. Gray is close to Grace, so I thought it would sound better. Like a real detective."

"You know you're completely nuts, don't you?"

As she flopped on my bed, she sighed, "I know, but it keeps life fun."

Hitting her with my pillow, I laughed. "You're right, what would I do without you?"

"Well, I think your life would be pretty boring."

"Yeah, you're probably right about that. Well, I do need your detective services."

"Great! You've come to the right place. What do you need?"

"I had another vision."

Grace lost all smiles and became very serious.

"Oh gosh, Cat, who was it?"

"Well, it was different this time. For the first time, it wasn't a kid. It was Mr. Williams."

"Mr. Who?"

Groaning, I knew the name I would have to use so she would know who I was talking about.

"One-Eyed, Scar Face."

"Oh! The janitor? He's scary!"

"I know. I mean, I always thought so too. I talked to him today, and he didn't seem too scary."

"You talked to him? He didn't suck your blood or anything?"

"What? No! He seemed... normal."

"Normal? From the monster?"

I scowled at her, so she added, "Okay, just tell me about the vision."

"He was just a kid, probably around your age. He and a friend had been playing basketball in their driveway. Then his ball went into the neighbor's yard, so he went after it."

"So, what's the big deal about that?"

"Well, the neighbor had a mean dog. As soon as Mr. Williams got his ball, he tried to run back home but the dog attacked him."

"What?" Grace leaned forward in shock.

"I know! It scared me! But you know what he yelled as the dog attacked him?"

"No. What?"

"He yelled, 'My eye! My face!'"

"What? No way! His face is that way because of a dog?"

"Yes."

"But I always thought..."

"I know what you always thought. We all thought the same thing."

"Cat, all I've ever heard was that he was a monster, and one Halloween night long ago, he came out of the grave and now worked at the school to scare us all!"

"I know! I always heard something like that too!"

"So, you're telling me he's a normal person?" Grace asked with the lift of an eyebrow.

I thought about that for a second. "Gosh, I think he might be. Everyone has treated him awful. But if he's not a monster, then do you think he might not be trying to scare us?"

"I don't know. But you said when you gave him that rag back, he was nice to you."

"Yeah, I don't think a monster would thank me and call me 'dear'." I scrunched my face in confusion.

"What if all those stories we heard from everybody aren't true?" Grace's face expression mirrored mine.

"Hmm, maybe that's what mom was saying rumors are."

"I'm not sure, but we've all been so mean to him. What do you think we could do?" Grace asked.

"I don't know, that's why I was wanting to tell you about it."

"Well, maybe we could try talking to him. *NOBODY* does that! He's too freaky looking!"

"That's a great idea. Maybe we could get the gang over and tell them about it."

"Great! Then there will be five of us being nice to him instead of the two of us."

"But, what do I say to the gang? They don't know about my visions."

"I don't know," my sister leaned over and patted my leg. "You figure that part out. I'm going to bake some cookies. If we're going to have friends over tomorrow, we'll need the sugar to think straight." With a wink, she jumped off my bed and headed out of my room.

"All that sugar is going to do, is give mom and dad a houseful of loud, hyper middle schoolers!" I yelled after her.

CHAPTER 3

The next day my friends were all sitting in my living room. Grace had already handed out the cookies she had made.

"Grace, I love M&M cookies!" Tyler shoved one into his mouth, "Thanks!"

Grinning, she responded, "No problem Tyler. I love them too."

It all turned quiet, and they all looked at me.

"So, what's up? What did you want to talk to us about?" Becky asked.

I could feel my hands getting sweaty, and suddenly that cookie felt like it was sitting in the pit of my stomach. How in the world was I going to tell them about my visions?

"Well... Um... You see..."

I began to explain to them about me falling out of our treehouse and hitting my head on a rock. Next, I had to tell them how the fall had caused me to be able to see into people's lives that had been bullied. The hardest part was telling them that I had seen visions of them. I didn't know if they would be mad at me or think I was nuts.

"So, wait," leaning forward Dallas stared at me, "you're telling me that you can see people's memories when you look at them?"

Wiggling my fingers together nervously, I quietly added, "Um, yeah. I do."

"No stinkin' way!" Dallas gasped as she slumped back onto the couch.

I couldn't tell what she was thinking. But I didn't have to wait long. She jerked up and looked right at me, "That's the coolest thing I've ever heard!"

Letting out the breath that I had been holding, I asked, "So, you're not mad at me?"

"Mad at you, are you crazy?"

"Well, actually I thought you guys might think I was."

Then Tyler piped in, "Crazy? I think it's awesome!"

"So, Cat, what can we do to help?" Excitement danced in Becky's eyes.

"Well, that's why we asked you to come over. I had another vision, and

Grace and I wanted to tell you guys about it."

I went on to tell them about Mr. Williams. When I was done, they all started to talk at once.

"Wait!" Dallas sat up straight, "I thought he lived in a cemetery and came out to scare kids at night!"

"I heard he worked at the school and every year he would take some kids and kill them on Halloween!" Becky exclaimed wide-eyed.

"Well, I heard he got into a fight with an alien and lost. That's why he looks like that!" Tyler punched his fist in the air, pretending to fight off an alien.

"Guys! What if we're wrong? What if he got attacked by a dog when he was younger, and he's *normal*?"

"Oh, how sad! But I don't understand. How could we have all heard such different stories about him?" Becky wondered sadly.

"I don't know, I thought everyone thought he got in a fight with an alien," Tyler said.

"Gosh, how do we find out which one is true?" Dallas asked.

"What if we tried talking to him on Monday? Then we could see for ourselves what he's like. If he's nice and doesn't attack us, then maybe we've been wrong," Tyler suggested.

"Tyler! He won't attack us. Cat said he was nice to her." Whipping her head around, Becky looked my way and asked. "Right, Cat? He won't attack us?"

"No. Well, at least I don't think so. He was really nice to me."

"Okay, then let's plan on talking to him at lunch on Monday."

"Sounds good, Dallas."

Just then my mom came into the room.

"Oh, hi, kids." Looking at Grace and me, she said, "I need you two to run up to the store and grab some eggs and milk. We're almost out."

"Sure, we'll all go." I looked at my friends, "Is that fine with you guys?"

"Yeah! Sounds like fun, let's go!" Tyler jumped to his feet.

Before we headed out, my mom told all of us to dress warm. Michigan Novembers could get really cold. She had heard there might be snow in the forecast.

"Snow, yay!" Becky exclaimed.

"Now, don't get too excited," she warned. "It's only November, so if we do get snow, it probably won't stick to the ground."

"Bummer," Shoulders slumped, Tyler zipped up his coat.

As we started walking to the store, I couldn't help but think about how different we all were from each other. But at the same time, we were becoming such great friends. Thinking back to our last hang out in the tree house, it had gotten really serious, and everyone was sharing stories of their struggles.

Becky had the happiest face I had ever seen. I used to think that no one could ever say anything to hurt her. Boy was I wrong. She ended up telling all of us how much it hurt her when people teased her. Being overweight made people feel free to say things that weren't nice. We kept reminding Becky of what a beautiful person she was on the inside.

I looked over and saw Dallas skipping. She was so happy, but her thick winter hat was pulled low over her forehead to help keep the warmth in. Her hair hadn't grown out enough to keep her head warm. She told us she'd been fighting cancer, but now she is in remission. Which meant she was doing really good. I could see she was getting stronger all the time, and it was great to see her skipping arm in arm with my sister down the sidewalk.

As we entered the store we headed straight for the milk and eggs. Dallas and Grace were still trying to skip in the store. They turned down an aisle, and I heard a sound.

"Oomph."

"Oh my gosh, we're so sorry," Grace and Dallas said at the same time.

As I rounded the corner, I saw that they had bumped into a man's back. As he slowly turned around, I saw their eyes widen as they realized who it was.

Dallas gulped, "Um, so sorry, Mr., um, Mr. Williams."

I noticed Grace slowly take a step back. With fear in her eyes, she managed to get words out of her mouth. "We're so sorry. We didn't mean to run into you."

But to our amazement, he smiled. Well, it looked more like a half-smile because the scar made his mouth tighter on one side. But he smiled, and said, "It's okay, kids. Just be careful."

Leaving us with our mouths hanging open he added, "I wouldn't want anything bad to happen to you, now would I?"

We all took deep breaths as we rushed out of the store after we had purchased our things for my mom. Even though running into Mr. Williams scared Grace, it didn't seem to cause her to forget her favorite candy. We left with a bulky bag of gummy worms.

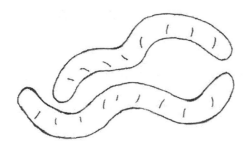

"Woah! That was crazy!"

"Yeah, what did he mean when he said he didn't want Dallas and me to get hurt? Was he kinda saying it in a scary way? Meaning, 'Look out kids! I don't want you to get hurt' but then he really plans on hurting us." With her fingers clinging to the worms, her hands flew in the air expressing her fear.

"Grace! He wouldn't hurt you. Come on, he sounded like he cared. Right, guys?" I asked.

"Um, well, I wasn't so sure. I got a little freaked out," Tyler giggled nervously, "but it's probably because of all the things we've heard about him."

"Yeah, let's give him a chance," Becky added. "Cat and Grace gave us a chance and look at our friendship now."

"Huh. You've got a point there," Dallas agreed. "Okay, let's do it!

As we walked back towards my house, my mind whirled. Will being nice to him bring us a new friend? Or will we not make it to high school alive?

CHAPTER 4

Monday morning came, and Grace and I hurried to get to school. After we left the store over the weekend, we all had agreed to meet up at lunch on Monday to see if we could spy on Mr. Williams. We wanted to see if we could ask him a few questions, but we had to do it without letting him know what we were up to.

Once we got to our first hour class, our teacher surprised us, "Class, take out your pencils, time for a pop quiz."

Groaning, I leaned over to my friend since kindergarten, and muttered sarcastically. "Great, Tiff. Just how I like to start the week."

Tiffany shrugged her shoulders and pulled out her pencil. We were not as close as we used to be. She didn't seem to like my new friends. She said she still wanted to hang out, but she wanted to stay friends with Holly and Amy.

They'd become the meanest girls in the whole 8th grade. We had all been best friends for a long, long time. But, since I won't be mean to others, I started to hang out with the "uncool" kids. Now my old friends wouldn't speak to me anymore. Except for Tiffany. And she only talks to me once in a while. Holly and Amy stick their noses up at me. I wish they'd be nicer to others. So far that hasn't happened.

After what felt like forever, first hour had only a couple minutes left. The bell was just about to ring, so we all began to walk towards the door to wait. Becky had started to talk about her questions for Mr. Williams.

"Wait, are you guys talking about One-Eyed Scar Face?"

"What? No, Holly, we're talking about Mr. Williams."

"Right, like I said. You mean the janitor?" she said with disgust. "Now why would anyone ever want to talk to him? I mean, he's a freak! His face looks like it should be in a horror movie." She leaned toward us and tried to talk in a scary voice, "I've heard he comes out at night and howls with the wolves. I bet that's why he stinks. He probably never showers."

"Oh, gross!" her friend, Amy, scrunched her face to encourage Holly to continue.

"I know, plus," she looked me straight in the face, daring me to challenge her, "I bet he's homeless. He sure looks and smells like it."

With my blood boiling, I clenched and unclenched my fists and opened my mouth to give Holly a piece of my mind when Dallas beat me to it.

"You know what, Holly, your words used to hurt me so much, but now? I see that being mean is the only way you know how to be. Well, guess what! Your words don't have to hurt me anymore. Instead of being hurt by you, I feel sorry for you."

"Ha, wait, me? You feel sorry for *me*? Why?"

I watched as Dallas got on her tiptoes, leaned in towards Holly, and quietly but with steel said, "Because deep down you must be a miserable person. As long as you hurt others you will never have true friends."

With that, she spun around and stormed off. Chasing her down the hall, I yelled, "Dallas, wait up!"

Dallas stopped and leaned against the wall, putting her hands on her bent knees. "I can't believe I did that!" As she rocked back and forth, she repeated, "I can't believe I just did that. I actually stood up to Holly."

"Yeah, you did. It was so awesome!"

"But I was so nervous. My body was shaking. My face was sweating, and everyone was watching!"

"I know! I think everyone thought it was so cool!"

"But Cat, don't you see? I'm becoming just as bad as her! She's so mean, and I was just as mean back!"

Thinking about her words, I responded. "Dallas, I don't think you have a mean bone in your body. You weren't trying to hurt her. You were letting her know that she hurts others and it has to stop."

"I know, she just started calling Mr. Williams names, and it made me so mad. I know how she has hurt Becky, Tyler, me, and now you too. I just lost it."

"Come on, maybe she'll think about what you said and will start being nice." Dallas gave me a 'whatever' look and grabbed my arm as we headed to our next hour.

I never thought lunchtime would come but it finally did. As I entered the already loud and crowded cafeteria, I met up with my friends. I had just sat down with my chicken sandwich and fruit, when I heard Tyler yell, "Hey guys, there he is!"

We all turned to see where Tyler was pointing. We watched as Mr. Williams slowly shuffled his feet while wiping a table that some kids had just left.

"Hey, let's go talk to him!" Becky jumped up from the table and started walking towards him.

"Hey, wait for us!" I choked out in the loudest whisper I could.

With my heart pumping, I couldn't wait. This was the moment. The moment I had been anxiously waiting for. We would find out if Mr. Williams was really a normal person, or were we doomed to find out he was the monster we had always heard him to be.

CHAPTER 5

We pretended we were throwing our napkins and straws into the trash can right next to him.

I wasn't sure how we were going to talk to him. I thought it could get a little awkward if we just stood there and stared at him.

"Hi, Mr. Williams! Isn't it a nice day?"

Chuckling, I whispered to Dallas, "Leave it to Becky to do the talking."

"Oh, hi kids." He looked over at Dallas and Grace. "Are you girls alright from the store the other day?"

Looking over I saw both girls were shaking their heads up and down.

Dallas found her voice and answered, "Yup, we're fine, thanks."

"Good, good. It sure would break my heart to think I hurt one of you girls."

We all looked at each other and realized he was serious. Maybe, just maybe, he wasn't going to try to eat us on Halloween night!

"We just threw our stuff away and saw you here, so we thought we'd say, hi."

Looking surprised, he responded, "Well that's awful nice of you kids. Did you have a nice weekend?"

"Oh, great!"

"Yup."

"Yeah," we all answered at the same time.

"What did you do this weekend?" Becky asked.

We all looked at him waiting for his answer, hoping to get some clues.

He just stood there scratching his chin. "Hmm, what did I do this weekend you ask?"

He turned his head to look at each one of us. As soon as he looked at me, once again my eyes connected with his one eye and I started to see stars...

Our very old Mr. Williams was leaning over, wiping a lunch table, when he heard a sixth-grade girl sniffling. He looked over, and there she was, sitting by herself crying. Lunch untouched.

He slowly walked over and sat across from her.

Talking in a calm voice not to scare her, he asked, "What's wrong, Sammy?"

She looked up with fear in her eyes.

He put up a hand to stop her from commenting.

"I know I look scary with my patch and this scar, but I'm just wanting to make sure you're okay."

She shook her head back and forth.

"Can you tell me what's wrong?"

She looked farther down the table to three girls who were laughing.

"They always tease me and call me names." She sniffed and wiped her runny nose with her sleeve.

"What do they say to you?"

"Well, today they called me fatty and said I looked like a big round tomato."

"Why did they call you a tomato?"

"Because, don't you see? I have red hair!"

The girl looked shocked that Mr. Williams didn't realize it.

"Oh. Is that supposed to be a bad thing?"

She rolled her eyes like he was from another planet.

"Yes! I hate my hair. Everyone laughs at it and calls me names. Not to mention my freckles!" After a pause, she added. "They tell me I'm ugly."

"Oh, I see. So," He paused and pretended to be thinking real hard.

"So, you're telling me because you have red hair and freckles that makes you ugly?"

Sadly, she answered, "Yes, and because I'm fat."

"Hmm, that's interesting."

"Why?"

"Because my wife's hair was red just like yours, and she had even more freckles than you. And guess what?"

Now he had her full attention.

"What?"

"I've always thought she was the most beautiful woman I had ever seen."

Now the girl's eyes were as round as quarters.

"Really?"

"Oh, yes, and do you know what I've always told her?"

"What?"

"I've always told her that *redheads are God's roses.*"

"Roses! I like that. Roses are so pretty."

Chuckling, he added, "And so are you. Don't believe what those girls are saying about you. And you know what else?"

"What?"

"They're probably just jealous."

"Of me. Why?"

"Because there's a certain boy over there that keeps looking your way. And I don't think it's because he thinks you're ugly or overweight. I think it makes those girls mad."

Looking over, she sees the boy he's talking about.

"Oh, but I don't like that boy."

"It doesn't matter. Looks like they do."

"Now finish up your eating and get outside to play. It's a beautiful day."

As he stands up, she says, "Mr. Williams?"

"Yes?"

"Thank you. And do you know what?"

"What?"

"I think it'd be nice if you brought your wife a red rose today, she might really like it."

"That's a great idea. I might just do that."

The next scene in my mind is Mr. Williams at the cemetery laying a red rose at the base of a tombstone.

As the vision cleared, I heard Mr. Williams answer, "What did I do this weekend? Hmm, let me see." After a long pause, he looked at us and said dreamily, "I did what I always do on weekends. I spent time visiting with my wife."

I gasped and took a step back. He was not a monster who was going to eat us. He wasn't going to come out on Halloween and kill us. No, he was a man who had a heart. A very kind heart that wanted to help others. The scars on his face were just an outward appearance. We all had let that determine who we thought he was. Why had we believed all those rumors about him? Well, let me tell you. We were wrong.

Dead wrong.

CHAPTER 6

The following day at recess, my friends and I were sitting together in a circle talking about Mr. Williams when I heard Tiffany holler out my name.

"Hey, Cat! Come on over, and let's shoot some hoops."

I turned to look at my friends, but they waved me off. "Don't worry, Cat, go play. We know you like basketball."

"I'll go, but why don't you guys join me? We can all play."

"Um, you have obviously never seen me try to play. I can't even dribble the ball!" Beck exclaimed wide-eyed.

I could see the panic in her eyes, so I thought of a different idea. "Okay, why don't you and Dallas watch us play. Tyler, you can come with me. I know you like basketball."

Shrugging, Tyler dug the toe of his shoe into the dirt. "I don't know, I don't think those kids will want me to play."

As I looked over at the courts, I saw that it was only the sporty kids shooting hoops. I turned back to Tyler, watching the glimmer of excitement in his eyes, as he looked at the courts. But it quickly darkened as the fear of going over there took a hold of him. I lifted my chin up high, grabbed his arm and pulled him over towards Tiffany.

"Yeah, thanks for asking Tiff. Tyler and I would love to play."

I watched as all the kids stopped playing.

"Um, Cat, we only have room for one more player." Looking at Tyler, Tiffany added, "Sorry, no room," and walked off bouncing the ball. "Hurry up, Cat, we're starting!"

With head down Tyler mumbled, "It's okay, Cat, I didn't want to play anyway."

"How dare she!"

Pulling on Tyler's arm, I walked up to them. "We will make room for Tyler. There are plenty of kids who can join to make the teams even."

"But, Cat, we—" Tiffany started.

"No, I won't play unless Tyler can play too."

"Fine," Trent, a boy in my class said as he walked over with a basketball tucked under his muscular arm. "He can play, but he's on your team. Us," as he motioned to all the sporty kids, "against you and whoever you can find to be on your team. You'll need at least three more people if it's you and Tyler."

"Fine, I'll make my own team. Be right back."

I twirled around and began marching around the basketball court, with a determined swing in my step. Catching up to me, Tyler asked, "What are you doing? We don't have to play."

"Are you kidding me? We sure are playing. We just need to find three more people."

"Anyone want to play?" I yelled out to no one in particular, hoping someone would answer.

I saw a girl wearing pink and purple polka-dot leggings talking to Becky and Dallas. She waved at me. "I will."

An already sweating, red-faced boy shyly raised his hand to volunteer.

"Great, see? Heather and Billy said they would play. We just need one more." As I looked around, I only saw one more kid on the side.

"Oh, shoot," I mumbled under my breath, "It's Timmy." Needing players though, I yelled out, "Hey Timmy, do you want to play?"

"Ha, you want Timmy the Toothpick?" Trent said. "He probably can't even lift the ball! Have you seen how skinny he is? He has absolutely *no* muscle to him. Good one, Cat, now you'll really win!"

"Yes, we want Timmy on our team, and quit calling him that name." As I snapped at Trent, I felt bad, because I realized I had called Timmy that name a lot before. We all called him Timmy the Toothpick because he was the tallest kid in our grade. Besides being tall, he was as skinny as a toothpick.

I looked over, and he slowly started to head over our way. As he walked, he kept his hands in his front pockets and looked at the ground, like he always did.

"Okay, guys, we only have fifteen minutes of recess left, so let's play some ball." I looked at our team and realized we would probably get creamed. We had Tyler, who was one of the smallest boys in our whole grade, and Heather, who wore glasses that were so thick they made her eyes look like owl eyes. Then there was Billy, who was sweating so bad just from walking across the playground. He was wearing a thin coat that looked two sizes too small. And that left of course, Timmy, who wouldn't even look at me when I was talking.

"Come on, Cat, let's get started. This should be fun!" And I heard the other team laughing.

"Come on guys, we can do this." I tried to encourage.

But as I walked over to play, I kept thinking about how much we were going to lose. It wasn't fair that they wouldn't split the teams up.

As we started the game, I threw the ball to Billy and he caught it. But just as quickly it fell out of his hands and the other team grabbed it and scored. After a couple of minutes, I called for a time out.

Huddling in our group I tried to give them ideas that would help us make at least one basket. As I was talking, I saw Timmy looking at his feet.

"Timmy, look at me. We need all of us working together."

Then it happened. He looked up at me with the saddest, most defeated look on his face. Our eyes connected, and I started to see stars...

Timmy was getting home from school one day, and he walked into his house. He looked around and shook his head. He grabbed a large trash bag and started picking up empty beer cans and bottles from

the kitchen. He walked into the living room where his dad was laying back snoring in his recliner. He continued to fill the bag, but the noise startled his dad awake.

Timmy stiffened, as I watched the vison in my head unfold, I realized why. As his dad tried to sit up, he looked at his son.

"Wh... what are you doing? I was trying to sleep!" he yelled while slurring his words.

Looking at the ground, Timmy answered, "S...sorry, Dad, I was just picking up before mom got home."

"What? Do you think I made a mess? Get over here!"

Scuffing his feet across the floor, Timmy slowly walked over to his dad. He grimaced as he waited for what would come next.

Slap! "That's for waking me up!"

Slap again! "That's for just being a loser. You will always be a good for nothing loser! Now get out of here!"

And before his dad could hit him again, Timmy dropped the bag and ran outside. He grabbed a basketball and started throwing it against the house as hard as he could while tears ran down his red, scared face.

After what seemed like forever, he took a deep breath, turned around and shot at his basketball hoop which was way far away.
And he swished it.

CHAPTER 7

"Oh my gosh!"

"What, Cat?"

I hadn't realized I had said that out loud. As I looked at Timmy, I could see a faint mark on his cheek, but you had to look really hard as it had faded over time.

"Hey, Cat! Time to play, or are you chicken?" Trent yelled out.

"Um." Trying to concentrate on the game, I came up with an idea. "Okay, guys, let's all spread out, and Timmy, why don't you stand back here," I said as I pointed to a spot that was not even close to the basket. "You will be farther away, so no one will block you back there. Tyler, you throw it to Timmy, and then he'll shoot."

"What?" Heather exclaimed. "That's way too far out!"

I looked, and to my amazement, her eyes were even rounder than before. "It's called a three-pointer, and we could use all the points we can get. Let's just try it, okay?"

"Okay," they all said, except for Timmy.

I looked at him as everyone else walked off. "I know it's far from the basket, but we just need some points, and you're the only one who hasn't shot yet. Just try." I made sure he was looking at me and added, "You can do it, Timmy."

The next play went exactly like I was hoping. No one was guarding Timmy that far back, and Tyler threw it to him. To everyone's amazement, the ball went in. It not only went in, but it was so smooth that it never hit the rim or backboard. All you could hear was the swoosh from the ball hitting the net. Everyone froze. Slowly, they all turned and looked at Timmy. Soon we heard screaming and cheering from the sidelines. I knew those voices. I turned and saw Dallas and Becky jumping up and down with arms just a flailing, cheering us all on.

Man, did I wish Grace was here to see this, but since she was in sixth grade, we only got to eat with her. She was already back in class.

"Beginners luck!" Trent hollered.

"We'll just see about that!" I yelled back. I quickly ran over to Timmy and asked, "Can you do that again?"

With a little shake of his head, and twitch of his mouth he answered, "Yeah, I can."

Speaking so only our team could hear, I answered back, "Then let's play ball, and kick some butt!"

"Yeah!" Billy said as he pumped the air with his fist, all the while sweat ran down his face like a waterfall.

"This is so exciting!" Heather exclaimed, eyes wide, and hands clasped under her chin, all the while a grin took over her face.

The last five minutes of the game went fast with our team winning by two points. Timmy made most of the baskets, except Tyler and I both made one.

When the bell rang, everyone who had ended up watching the game, which ended up being half the kids outside, all ran up to Timmy and congratulated him. I heard some kids telling him he did a great job. Some added how cool he was, while still others told him he should go out for the basketball team. As we slowly walked back to the school, I watched as all the kids surrounded Timmy. There was something different about him. He had the faintest hint of something. Just the tiniest, but there was no mistake.

Timmy was smiling.

CHAPTER 8

Later that night, I sat Indian style on my bed with math papers sprawled out all over my covers. I had so much homework, and I wasn't going to get it done if I couldn't get past this question. My mind kept drifting back to the basketball game earlier today. I had to concentrate on my homework. I kept punching in numbers on my calculator, but I knew I wasn't getting the correct answer.

"Ugh! I can't get it!"

Boy, did I hate math, or maybe it hated me. I had been stuck on this problem for fifteen minutes now. Just as I threw my calculator onto my bed in frustration, I heard my phone ding.

Leaning over to my nightstand, I snatched it up.

I was shocked to see a text from Holly. She hadn't been texting me since I started hanging out with Tyler, Becky, and Dallas.

Curiosity took over, so I clicked on it. My heart sank.

HOLLY: *You are now officially a loser! I mean come on, Cat. I saw you playing basketball today. Can someone say, "Geek fest!" I mean a team of Timmy, Billy, Tyler, Heather and you? What were you thinking? You're the joke of the whole school now. You should hear what everyone is saying about you. You just went from 'totally popular' to 'biggest loser'! Now guess what? NOBODY LIKES YOU ANYMORE!*

As I sat on my bed, I felt the tears start to burn the back of my eyes. Why was Holly like this? Why didn't I see it before? I mean, I'd been friends with her for so long. Had she always been like this? Thinking back, I realized she had always talked about others behind their backs, but it got a lot worse once she got her phone.

Just then Grace skipped into my room, singing at the top of her lungs. As soon as she saw my tears, which had finally escaped and now ran down my cheeks, she froze. Singing instantly came to a halt, and her feet were planted on the ground. Her legs seemed to go from standing still to racing in a second. She ran over and hugged me as tightly as she could.

"Oh my gosh! What's wrong?"

I was so embarrassed that I had been crying, that I tried to push her away.

"Oh, no you don't, Cat!" She tried to hug me even tighter. "Tell me what's wrong."

"I will if you..."

"What? I can't hear you."

Twisting my head to the side so I could actually breathe, I tried again. "I said, I will if you let go, your squishing me!"

"Oh." She quickly released her hold on me. "Oops, sorry. I guess I saw you crying and freaked out. What's wrong?"

I held my phone out and let her read the text.

I watched as her expression changed from shock, to hurt, then anger. After a minute, she put my phone on my bed and sat down next to me.

"Don't listen to her."

"I know, but she said everyone..."

"Stop, Cat." Grace said shaking her head from side to side. "Don't you tell everyone else not to listen or believe anything Holly says? Besides, it isn't true."

"You're right. It's easy to tell someone else not to listen to her, but as soon as I saw those mean words I just broke down. Man, it's hard not to let those words hurt."

"I know. And it can be hard not to believe them. But listen. What she said isn't true. I didn't have to wait until I got home to hear about your little basketball game today. No, *everyone* was talking about it."

Groaning, I buried my face into my hands. "Great. I'm the laughing stock of the whole school."

"No, that's what I'm trying to tell you. Everyone was talking about how cool it was. They all loved it. I even had some kids tell me they thought you were so awesome!"

"What? Really? That's not what Holly said." As soon those words came out, I covered my mouth with my hand. "Oops, sorry. You're right. I can't believe what she says."

"You know what? I used to not like who you became when you hung out with your old friends. I actually couldn't stand you. I always hoped that I would never act or be like you. Your friends were all jerks to me. But this year, you've changed, for the better. So much better. I know you and your old friends thought you were *so much cooler* than everyone else. It's almost as if Holly, Amy, and Tiff think that the meaner they are to people, the cooler it makes them. But you know what I think of you now?"

"What?" I asked, kinda scared of what the answer might be.

"Standing up for the kids that get picked on, and even becoming friends with them, has made you the *coolest* person I know." After a pause, she added, "And now ..." she made sure I was paying attention, "I want to be *just like you.*"

CHAPTER 9

Earlier in the week, Becky had asked if we all wanted to go to her house after school on Friday. I could feel myself getting nervous, when the day finally arrived. I was excited to go to her house, so we could all hang out, but nervous because Becky always rode the bus every day. That meant I had to ride her bus.

Now, being in the eighth grade, you'd think I'd be used to it by now. To be honest though, I'd been a walker my whole life. The only couple of times that I rode the bus was for field trips and with Tiffany and Amy to their houses a couple of times. Becky, on the other hand, said she had to ride the bus for almost an hour every day. That's a long time!

As the last bell rang for the day, I grabbed my backpack and met up with my friends. We had decided to meet by a tree right outside the school, so we could get on the bus together.

"Hey, Cat, this is so exciting, we never get to ride the bus!"

As I glanced over at my sister, I opened my mouth to tell her that it probably wouldn't be as much fun as she thought. But, I could see the happiness on her face, so I clamped my lips together and stayed quiet.

"Okay, guys. It's bus number 18. Let's go."

Following Becky, with my heart feeling like it was in a race, I thought it would beat right out of my coat. I slowly climbed each step up to what could be the worst hour of my life. I handed the bus driver my pass and continued to follow Becky down the aisle. I found that the bus was packed, and kids were screaming a million different things across rows of seats. Their arms were flailing, and their heads bobbed up and down. I couldn't believe how loud it was. Becky stopped suddenly, and I almost slammed into her.

"Evan, can I sit here please?"

"No," he set his backpack on the seat next to him, "It's saved."

"But there's not a lot of seats left."

Leaning forward, he said to Becky, "If this was the last seat on the bus, I wouldn't let you sit with me." Looking her up and down with a face full of disgust, he added, "Um, I think the only way you'd fit into a seat anyways is if you had a whole seat to yourself."

I started to hear snickering from the other kids around me.

My racing heart was now pounding, not because of fear, but because I was angry. I leaned past Becky, so Evan could see me.

"Cat! What are you doing on the bus?"

"I'm going to Becky's house, and she and I need a place to sit, so if you would kindly move over so Becky can sit with you, we would greatly appreciate it."

As he looked at me, I could tell he was getting frustrated. Sneering he responded, "She is not sitting with me," adding, "but you can sit with me, Cat."

Tiffany and Holly had always said they thought Evan liked me. Well, if this was how he treated people, there was no way I would ever like him back. He could look somewhere else.

"Evan, Becky asked to sit with you. I didn't."

"Hey," the bus driver barked sternly into the intercom. "What's the holdup? Everyone, sit down."

"Fine!" Evan snapped. He grabbed his backpack and pushed his way past Becky, but not before sending her tumbling into me. Luckily, I grabbed the seats on both sides of me and kept us from falling on our rear ends.

"You guys can have this seat, I'll get a better one."

I watched as he marched down the aisle and sat with Sidney, a girl in my grade.

As I scooted in next to Becky, I asked, "What was that all about?"

She shrugged like she was used to it. "On days when it's full, I have to sit with someone else, and that's how most respond to me. It's no big deal."

Staring at her, I found myself so angry, not at her, but at Evan. "It *is* a big deal, Becky. They shouldn't do that to you."

"Cat," I heard Dallas call my name. I had completely forgotten about everyone else because I was so mad. I looked forward and noticed that Dallas and Tyler were sitting right in front of us. They had three people in their seat, and they looked extremely scrunched.

"What?" I asked.

"It happens all the time. You just don't ride the bus."

"No, I've ridden the bus with Tiff and Amy and it never happened to them."

They all looked at each other, then towards me, with the look of pity. It all of a sudden hit me. It didn't happen to Tiffany or Amy because they were popular, and everyone liked them. Whereas the kids I was with now, were the ones people labeled as the oddballs, weird kids, kids that just don't fit in. Whatever people wanted to call them.

I lifted my chin a little higher and sat a little straighter and added, "Well, it shouldn't be that way."

"Cat, it just is. Nothing you can do about it. Don't worry, we're used to it," Tyler responded.

"Hmph." I slouched back in my seat and crossed my arms, "Well, I'm not happy about it."

Fifteen minutes later, the bus was beginning to clear out. Tyler and Dallas were laughing at something Grace had said as she leaned into the aisle across from them. Becky was unusually quiet, so I just leaned back in my seat to rest.

That's when I heard it.

Some snickers, then very faintly, "Hey fatty, what did you eat for breakfast yesterday? Because it's still hanging on you. Have you ever thought about going on a diet? You sure need one."

I wouldn't have heard it if I hadn't laid my head back against the seat. And it continued. I couldn't hear all of it, but I got an idea by the broken-up words they were saying. "So, fat...die...big as a pig...oink, oink."

I turned to look at Becky to see if she had heard them. I couldn't see her face because she was leaning against the window. I slowly bent forward until I could see one single tear running down her round cheek.

Yup, she could hear them. I whipped around in my seat and snapped at the seventh-grade boys behind me.

"Knock it off! You're just big jerks!"

"Ha! You call us big, have you looked at your friend? Wait, of course you have. She's so big you couldn't miss her even if you tried!" Slugging each other, thinking they were so funny.

Now I was so furious, I thought I was going to explode.

"Hey idiots." I was just about to tell them off when I felt someone gently but firmly grab my arm. I whipped around to find a red rimmed, puffy-eyed Becky shaking her head at me.

"Don't, Cat. It won't do any good. I can handle it."

"But it's not true!" My high-pitched voice squeaked in desperation. "It's not right." My own eyes began to cloud with tears.

"I'm used to it. And even if they stopped today, they would just do it again later."

I saw a slight smile begin to form on her lips. "But, thanks for sticking up for me." Looking down at her lap she added, "I've never had anyone do that for me before."

She looked at me and our eyes connected. I started to see stars...

CHAPTER 10

Becky was sitting on her bed with a bunch of books tossed all around her. Grabbing one, she started to flip through it, only to toss it back on the bed and grab a different one. She continued that cycle until she got so frustrated that she pushed them all off her bed. She flopped her body completely flat onto her bed and buried her face into her pillow and sobbed.

After some time went by, she wiped her tears and walked over to a mirror that hung on the back of her bedroom door. Next, she twirled around and looked at herself from every angle.

"It didn't work!" she yelled. She yanked the mirror off the door. "Stupid mirror!" In the process, she almost tripped over one of the books she had pushed off her bed.

"Ouch! My toe!" She plopped herself down onto the floor. Grabbing a book, she began to sob while holding it up in front of her, while yelling at it. "You didn't work! You didn't work! I tried SO hard! You lied to me!" Continuing to cry she began to take deep breaths to try to calm herself.

Next, she got on her hands and knees and began to collect all the books she had bought. She walked over to her trash can and dumped them in with a large thud. But not before I could get a glimpse of the titles. They were not just any ordinary books. The titles were *How to Lose 40 lbs. in a Week*, *Look Skinny Like Me in Only 30 Days!* and so on. No, they were not just reading books for fun.

They were diet books.

She turned and left her room with shoulders slumped and tears streaming down her rosy cheeks.

The vision ended, and I realized something. Becky had been right. I couldn't make those boys stop. Even if they did, someone else would be teasing her sooner or later. As I looked at my friend and saw the hurt in her eyes, I realized something I *could* do.

Today, I would be nice to her. Today, I would be her friend. It was my choice. Today, tomorrow, the next day. Then the day after that, and every day that followed. I *could* make a difference. So, I took a deep breath and told her what I thought she needed to hear.

"Becky, what those guys were saying, it's not true. They think they're better than you, but they aren't." I paused, trying to remember what my mom always said to Grace and me. "My mom always told us that we were no better than the nerdiest kids, but the most popular kids were no better than us. Some kids just don't realize that you're a great person, and they would be lucky to have you as their friend. They are truly the ones missing out. You don't have to or need to change. I mean look at our friends."

We turned and looked. They were all busy laughing not realizing what was going on. Grace's mouth was moving a mile a minute, while her hands were going every which way as she told one of her crazy stories. Dallas's head was thrown backward, and Tyler was leaning forward holding his stomach, both with laughter bubbling from deep within.

"We," I continue, "like you just as you are. Please don't change."

She wrapped me in a big bear hug and squished my face into her arms. "Um, Becky, I can't breathe!"

"Oops," she pulled away and grinned from ear to ear. "Sorry I just couldn't help myself. Thank you, Cat."

"For what?"

"For everything, but mainly for just being my friend."

"You bet, but I should be the one thanking you."

She looked at me with a question in her eyes.

"I needed your friendship just as badly as you needed mine. So, thanks for being my friend."

Just then Grace yelled, "Hey, Becky, there's your house! Are we next?"

As the bus began to slow down, Becky started to stand, "Yup, this is our stop." She turned and looked at me while talking to all of us, and added, "Let's go guys. Let's go have some fun."

CHAPTER 11

Monday came way too fast. We all had so much fun at Becky's house on Friday. We ended up telling funny stories. I wasn't as good at it, but man, Grace, Tyler, and Dallas had us crying, we were laughing so hard.

Sighing, I slowly crawled out of bed. Mondays were still my least favorite day of the week. Give me a Friday or Saturday any day, but Mondays? I could pass on those.

Going through my morning routine, I got dressed, brushed my teeth and hair, and headed down stairs at a slower pace than normal. Sitting down I ate my chocolate sugar cereal, covered in cold whole milk.

I was surprised when we got to school on time. My friends and I all decided to meet up at lunch to talk about another game of basketball. I hadn't told anyone about my vision of Timmy, but I couldn't wait to find him and see if he wanted to play on our team again.

Sitting at the lunch table, Tyler couldn't stop talking about how we had beat the jocks the week before. Looking around, we spotted Timmy sitting alone.

"Hey, guys, I'll be right back. I'm going to ask Timmy if he'll play again."

"Okay. Beg him if you have to!" Dallas yelled over her shoulder as I walked away.

Spotting him across the cafeteria, I walked up and asked him, "Hey, Timmy, would you like to play basketball again after you're done eating?"

"Um," still looking down at the table, "I'm not sure."

"Why not? You're fantastic!"

That caught his attention, and he looked up at me. Our eyes connected, and I started to see stars...

It was last week, and we had just finished with the basketball game at lunchtime. So many kids were telling Timmy he should go out for

the team. He had gotten back to class, when Trent and Holly walked up to him.

"Hey, loser. Beginner's luck," Trent smirked.

"Yeah, how could you be good at anything? I hear your dad's the town drunk. You'll probably turn out just like him."

Trent swatted Holly's arm, "Ha, that's a good one, Holl."

She batted her eyes at Trent, "Thanks."

They turned to walk off, but Trent paused, turned back to Timmy and added, "And don't even think about going out for the basketball team." He leaned down and put both hands on Timmy's desk, got in his face and continued, "If you do, I'll make it miserable for you."

"Don't worry, Trent, look at him. His life is probably miserable already. Drunk dad and crazy as a freak!"

"Yeah, you're right, Holly. Let's go." They walked off together, never looking back.

Just then a boy from recess ran up to Timmy, waving a sheet of paper. "Here, Timmy! Here's the signup sheet for basketball. You've got to do it!"

Pushing it away, Timmy answered, "No, just forget it."

"Forget it? Are you crazy? You're awesome! You'll for sure make the team. You're the best we've got."

Jumping up from his desk, he shoved the sheet of paper back at the boy and almost knocked him over. "I said NO!" and he ran out of the classroom.

I just stood there staring.

"Cat, I'm not playing."

I quickly sat down next to him. I didn't care if he got mad at me. I wanted to talk to him.

"Timmy."

"And please, stop calling me that. Call me Tim." After a long pause, he said, "I *hate* the name Timmy."

"Oh gosh, okay. I can do that." I added, "You know what? Tim fits you much better."

That made him sit a little taller.

"Listen, Tim. I'm not sure why you won't play, but I want you to know that there are a lot of kids who think you play awesome, me included. I think a lot of them look up to you."

"Look up to me? You've got to be kidding. Do you know who you're talking to?"

"Yes, I know exactly who I'm talking to. I'm talking to Tim. A nice kid in our grade who would never hurt a soul. And who happens to *kill* in basketball."

"But Trent and Holly...."

"Stop right there." I put my hand up to silence him. "They think so highly of themselves and think they are better than everyone else. One thing I have learned this year is to *never* believe anything they say." I shook my head, "Trent is just jealous of you. He has always been the best on the team, but you're making him nervous." With a slow grin, I added, "Let's play after we eat and give him a real reason to be nervous."

I stood up and started to walk off, but paused and added, "Then you can sign up for the basketball team. It starts soon, the first game is next week."

I left him shaking his head back and forth, but not before I saw his lips slowly turn upwards.

CHAPTER 12

Walking back to our lunch table, I passed Mr. Williams. Before, I would have made sure I kept my distance and walked as far away from him as I could. Now, I passed him with a smile and waved, "Hi, Mr. Williams."

He looked up from the floor he was mopping and replied, "Hello, Cat, hope you're having a nice day."

Wow, he knew my name! I had no idea. I answered him, "Yup, having a great one, hope you are too."

I continued to walk on because I couldn't wait to tell my friends that Tim was going to play. But the scene in front of me was anything but happy. My friends were all looking at their phones. Their cheeseburgers were pushed to the side and forgotten. I stopped to look at them before they saw me. Dallas looked over at Tyler's phone and shook her head. She was mad. Tyler kinda shrunk back into his shell. I noticed he would do that whenever someone picked on him. When I studied Becky, her face was flushed, and she looked like she was going to burst into tears. I looked around and figured Grace must have had to get back to class, because she was nowhere to be seen.

I walked right up to them and asked, "What's wrong?"

At the same time, all three laid their phones down and answered. "Nothing."

Becky tried to wipe the evidence of her tears away, while Tyler looked down at the table.

"We're just not hungry," he mumbled.

I planted my hands on my hips and tapped my toes, "Give it to me guys. What's going on?"

They all looked at each other. None of them wanted to be the one to have to tell me.

"Give me one of your phones." I begged, "Please."

Becky slowly pushed hers toward me.

I grabbed it and scrolled until I found what the problem was.

HOLLY: *Guys, do you actually think Cat wants to be your friend? She only feels sorry for you. She calls me all the time to tell me that she's only nice to you because you have no friends. She wishes she could hang out with me again. She is SOOOO over you guys. YOU GUYS ARE ALL SUCH LOSERS. (Her words, not mine). Sorry, but thought you should know the truth about Cat. Did you really think someone as popular as Cat would want to hang out with someone like you? Get real. You guys aren't worth it.*

"What! I didn't say that!"

I looked around and only saw hurt on their faces.

"Guys, are you really going to believe her over me?"

"Well, she's kinda right. You are a lot cooler than us. Why would you want to hang out with us anyway?" Becky murmured sadly.

"Come on, guys. Really? Have you not learned anything yet about Holly?" I chose to speak slowly so they heard every word. "She is full of lies. She'll say anything to hurt you. She doesn't care about what is right or wrong. She's just jealous and mad because I would rather hang out with you guys instead of her. You guys may not be as "cool" in Holly's eyes, but to me? You guys are *way* cooler."

They all just stared at me. I was kind of hurt that they didn't believe me. I twirled around to leave but heard Dallas call after me.

"Cat!"

As I turned around, she fumbled to get out of her seat, then walked over to me. She looked straight at me and said, "I believe you."

I couldn't help myself. I gave her a huge hug. "Thanks, Dallas."

"Okay. You can quit hugging me!" I pulled away, as a smile played at her lips.

With an idea forming in my head, I told her, "I'll talk to Holly and tell her...."

Shaking her head at me, she interrupted. "No, you don't have to do a thing. We believe you. If you make a scene, she'll get what she wants. It will give her an excuse to tell more lies. Actually, it will probably make her madder if she sees her words aren't going to hurt us. She's not going to break our friendship."

By now, Becky and Tyler had joined us. "Yeah, Dallas is right. You don't have to say a thing. We know you're our friend."

"Thanks, Tyler."

My eyes roamed to Becky. Wiping more tears, she let out a long breath, "Sorry I cried. I let myself believe it at first but realized what a lie it all was. Sorry I doubted you."

"That's what bullies do. They know your weak spot and will do anything to hit it. It's fine, Becky. I'm just glad you believe me."

"I do believe you. And you know what?"

"What?"

"I'm putting my stupid phone away. All it does is cause me pain."

And we walked out together. Those lies Holly had texted could have pushed us apart, but it backfired and made us stronger.

CHAPTER 13

We headed out for recess, and there was Tim, Billy, and Heather all waiting for us. As we got closer, I saw that Billy already had sweat running down his face, and Heather had her owl looking glasses on. But today, her eyes were full of excitement. She had added a hot pink head band, to match her coat and multi-colored striped leggings. I could only smile at this group. We must look like quite the team.

I heard Dallas and Becky on the sideline already cheering for us. What a crazy year this had been so far. But so much better than I could have ever imagined.

"Hey, guys, are you ready to eat our dust today?" Trent said as he came up to us.

His eyes bore into Tim's. Trent had to actually tilt his head up to see into Tim's eyes. "Are you sure you want to play? You may pay for it later."

I was just about to stand up for Tim when he surprised me and answered for himself.

"Just try. You don't scare me."

Trent stared back and puffed out his chest, "You sure about that?"

Standing at his full six foot, three inches Tim responded, "Yeah, I am."

Trent walked off or stormed off was more like it. We all stared at Tim. Billy said, "Oh, wow, Tim! That was sooo cool!"

Tim looked at me and said under his breath, "Come on, Cat. Let's beat them."

I just grinned and yelled to the other team, "We're ready!"

Boy, were we ready! We started by throwing Tim the ball every time, but the other team caught on and started putting two people on him, and no one on either Heather or Billy.

I called a timeout, and we all huddled together.

"Any ideas, guys? We're ahead by four points, but they're catching up."

"I've got two people on me. Billy, do you know how to set a screen?" Tim asked.

"Um, the only screens I know of are attached to my front door at home or on my phone."

I had to smile at that.

"Guys?"

We all looked at Heather.

"Uh," shifting her glasses farther up her nose she meekly said, "I know what a screen is." She shyly looked at Tim. "I sometimes watch basketball with my brother and dad. I'll set one for you."

Tim smiled and nodded his head toward her. "Sounds good. Thanks, Heather." Suddenly she turned two shades redder.

"Okay. Let's try the screen, but if it doesn't work then pass it to Tyler or Cat. They both can play pretty good too."

Just when I didn't think Tyler's smile could get any bigger, Tim looked at him and asked, "You're trying out for the team, right?"

"Uh, I don't think so. I'm way too short."

"Are you kidding me? You can handle the ball better than any of us. They're going to need a point guard."

Tyler just stood there, speechless.

"I'll tell you what. If you go out for the team, I will too."

I started laughing, because Tyler's feet were still planted in the same place, with his mouth hanging open. I could tell Tim had just given Tyler a huge compliment.

I heard a squeak come out of Tyler, "Okay."

We all laughed, Tim included. We went back to the game, ready to play.

I threw Tyler the ball, and he dribbled down the court. He watched as Heather set a screen for Tim. Tim ran to the side, and Tyler quickly passed it to him. To our excitement, Tim ran in for a layup just as the bell rang.

We were all screaming. I turned to look for Dallas and Becky, but they had a huge group around them cheering. I watched as the whole group on the side lines started running our way. I spotted them and saw that Becky's arms were flying every which way, her eyes lit up like a Christmas tree. I looked over at Trent's team, but they didn't look happy. Nope, not one bit. They were mad.

I thought I better go tell them that they did a good job. As I started walking over, I saw Tim had the same idea.

As we reached them, Tim held out his hand. "Good job, guys."

I added, "Yeah, good job."

Trent looked at Tim's hand, turned, and walked away. Tiffany looked at me and scowled. She whipped around and followed Trent.

I looked at Tim, and he shrugged his shoulders.

"Come on, it's time for class."

I started walking back and everyone joined us.

"Oh, my word, guys! That was so exciting!" Becky said.

I looked at her with a question on my face.

She looked down at the ground shyly. "Um, Dallas and I kinda lost our voices by screaming so much."

I turned to Dallas, and she croaked out, "Yeah, she's right. But it was so worth it."

As we walked back, I kept thinking about how much fun I had.

When we reached the doors that led inside, I heard Tim ask Tyler, "So, did you decide if you're going to try out or not? I just need to know if I should go in and sign up."

"Um, I'll try out. But don't be surprised if I don't make it."

"Oh, you'll make it. I watched the team last year. They could really use a good point guard."

I leaned over and whispered to the girls, "Guys, if they make the team, let's go to all the games and cheer them on."

"Yes!" Becky exclaimed.

"Great!" Dallas grabbed her throat. "But I'm going to have to get a whole bag of sore throat lozenges!"

CHAPTER 14

The following Tuesday night, Becky, Dallas, Grace and I met up at my house.

"Wow, isn't it great that Tyler and Tim both made the basketball team?" exclaimed Becky.

"Yeah, and we get to go watch them play!"

We had spent the last hour in my room, painting our faces and making posters for their first basketball game. Poster boards and markers were lying all over my bed. Paint and paintbrushes were scattered over my dresser, and boy, were we so excited to go cheer them on.

As my mom drove us to the school, I looked in the back seat to tell them something, but I just started laughing.

"What?" Grace asked.

"You guys look like that cartoon we used to watch, with your blue faces."

"Have you looked at yourself in the mirror?"

"Yes, but that's why I did half my face white and the other half blue." I replied.

Grinning at them, I noticed we were pulling into the parking lot.

"Okay, kids. Have fun. I'll pick you up when the game is over."

"Thanks!" We all yelled as we jumped out of the car.

As we entered the gym, we could see the team warming up.

"Oh, guys," Dallas pointed. "There they are."

Sure enough, there was Tim and Tyler with the team, shooting around.

"Let's go find some seats." Grace suggested.

As we sat down, Becky started to giggle.

"What's so funny?" I asked.

"Oh, nothing. I've just never been to a basketball game before. This is so fun!"

"What?" All three of us asked, whipping our heads around to look at her.

"What do you mean you've never been to a basketball game before?" Grace asked with her eyes widening.

"Well," She got a little embarrassed and looked down. "I guess I never had anyone to go with, so I just didn't go."

Not wanting her to feel bad, I answered. "Then you're in for the time of your life."

"Yeah, I love going to games!" Grace exclaimed.

"Guys," Dallas said. "Quit talking and watch. The game's going to start."

Sure enough, there stood Tim in the middle of the floor, getting ready to tip the ball to a teammate.

We were all on our feet excited to see if he would reach the ball before the other team did.

"Yay!" Dallas cheered as Tim slapped the ball to a teammate.

After a few minutes, we all sat down. I was having such a good time.

Usually, I sat with Holly, Amy, and Tiffany. Holly and Amy would just talk about boys the whole time. Tiff and I liked to watch the game, but we would just sit there. There was no jumping up and yelling, we were too cool for that.

I was sitting at a game with my face painted and a poster ready to hold up. Tyler was running down the court, dribbling extremely fast. He spotted Tim and threw it to him. Tim quickly turned, looked at the basket, and released the ball into the air. The ball looked like it was sailing, smooth and perfect. It went in with only the *swoosh* of the net. He made a three-pointer right as the loud, halftime buzzer was going off.

I was just about to jump up and scream with the rest of my friends, but I glanced over, and Holly, Amy, and Tiffany were looking at me in disgust, shaking their heads. For a moment, I paused and felt very dumb for how I was dressed and for having a big poster. I stayed sitting down and looked at my feet. I thought I didn't care anymore what they thought about me, but I guess I still struggled a little.

"Cat!" Becky yelled. As I looked her way, I saw the most joy on her face that I had ever seen. "Come on, this is a blast!"

Taking one more look toward my old friends, I let out a big sigh and slowly started to stand. Before I knew it, I got this funny feeling inside of me, and excitement started to bubble up in my chest. The next thing I knew, I was joining in on the fun. I began waving my poster high into the air, and of course, screaming at the top of my lungs, along with my friends.

Holly, Amy, and Tiffany could look at me like I was strange. Who cares. I was having the time of my life.

Since it was halftime, the team went into the locker room. Tim and Tyler had done a fantastic job. Our team was ahead by ten points. No one could stop Tim from making baskets, or swishing baskets was more like it.

Then, all of a sudden there was a commotion by the gym doors.

"What's going on?" Dallas asked.

"I don't know," I said, stepping on my tippy toes to look past everyone so I could see what was happening.

"Looks like a guy is trying to get into the game, but Mr. Holman won't let him in."

Sure enough, I could see our principal standing in the doorway with his back towards us, holding his hand up, keeping a man from entering the gym.

"Who is it? Can you tell? Why won't they let him in?" A million questions leaving Becky's mouth all at the same time.

"I don't know who it is," Grace replied. "But he's yelling and making a scene."

The guy looked familiar to me, but I couldn't remember where I had seen him before.

Just then the team came out of the locker room and the guy yelled. "Timmy! Timmy!"

With our principal still holding the guy back, I turned and saw Tim's facial expression change from excitement to shock when he heard his name being called out. His shoulders stiffened, and his face turned ghostly white. He instantly walked over to the side where his team sat during the game and plopped down. He put his head down towards his knees and stared at the floor.

That is when it hit me. Tim's dad. The reason the guy looked familiar was because I had seen him in my vision of Tim.

"Guys, who is that?" Dallas asked.

Gulping, I answered, "It's Tim's dad."

"Why's he being so loud?" Grace asked.

"Because," I said. "It's Tim's dad. His drunk dad."

CHAPTER 15

"Oh no!" Becky exclaimed as tears started to form in her eyes.

"Becky! Your tears are leaving streaks down your face. It's taking your paint off!" Grace exclaimed.

"Oh, I don't care. It's so sad."

"I know," Still not being able to take my eyes off the commotion by the doors.

"Look, guys, they're walking his dad out. They made him leave." Dallas told us, pointing to the gym doors.

The buzzer went off, signaling the beginning of the second half, but the atmosphere in the gym had totally changed.

Tim was on the floor playing, but everyone could tell he wasn't concentrating. Tyler threw Tim the ball, and Tim took a shot. It bounced hard off the backboard and flew to the left. And this was how the rest of the game went. Tim only made one basket in the third quarter. He had lost all focus. The coach ended up pulling him out for the last quarter.

"Look, guys, Tim looks so sad," Becky said, pointing his way.

"I know, that's gotta be so hard."

"I sure hope this doesn't give Trent and Holly any more reason to pick on him. I'll be so mad!" Dallas fumed.

"Yeah, I know. Me too." I nodded.

As the game ended with our school losing by four points, the whole team walked into the locker room with defeated faces. They all knew they could have won, if it had gone as well as it had in the first half.

We headed down the bleachers and walked to the middle of the floor. We waited for the team to come out. Slowly, boys started to exit the locker room. As soon as we saw Tyler, we rushed over and told him what a good job he had done. I noticed that he had looked defeated and had shrunk back into his shell. I had only seen him do that when he was being picked on.

"What's wrong?" I asked.

As he shrugged his shoulders, he said, "Nothing."

"Tyler, come on. It was a good game. You guys almost won," Dallas said, trying to lift his spirits.

Just then, he looked up and our eyes connected. I started to see stars...

The team had just lost the game, and they were all in the locker room listening to the coach give a speech. As soon as he was done, all the boys went to change and grab their bags.

After Tyler and Tim both got dressed, they started stuffing their jerseys in their bags. At that time, both their phones dinged within seconds of each other. They looked at one another and grabbed their phones.

First Tyler scrolled and found the new text.

TRENT: Hey shorty. You really suck, you know that, right? Do you realize you're the shortest on the team? And what happened to you? I thought with your dark skin you were supposed to be able to jump high and run fast, but nope! We white kids outshined you today. You got no height, no talent. You got nothing! Go back to sixth grade, where you belong...... Idiot.

Tyler then sank onto the closest bench and looked completely hopeless. Like he believed every. single. word.

Then Tim's Text:

TRENT: What the heck happened out there? You actually did halfway decent the first half. So, what changed? Oh, I know. Some loser's dad showed up completely wasted. Now that has got to be the most embarrassing thing I've ever seen. Too bad you're going to end up just like him.

Next time, don't bother to show up for the game. We all saw how you really play. Coach had to pull you out because you were so bad. Face it.

Your dad's a complete loser.

You're a complete loser.

I sucked in a breath and tried to hold back tears.

"Where's Tim now?" Grace asked, as she looked around the gym but couldn't find him.

"He's still in the locker room."

I turned my head and saw Tim walk out of the locker room doors but didn't look up. He just started to walk toward the exit.

"Good job, Tim!" Grace hollered.

"You did great!" Becky yelled as they rushed over to catch up with him.

"Thanks." He mumbled, still not looking at anyone or anything.

Tyler had found his mom in the stands and started that way. I hadn't moved a muscle. Why did people have to be so mean? If Trent didn't like Tim and Tyler, then so what? Why did he have to say mean things, though?

I didn't know what to do. I had really thought that if I just started being nice to people I had visions of, then everyone would be happy. Boy, was I wrong. This was so much deeper and harder than what I had expected. Like when Becky was on the bus, I couldn't stop the bullies. It didn't matter how nice I was, the people just kept bullying.

I watched as Tim and Tyler both walked out of the gym doors, towards the parking lot, looking completely lost.

Grace, Dallas, and Becky ran up to me. They all started to talk at once.

I couldn't listen to them right now. "Guys," I said, feeling like a loser myself because I couldn't fix it. "It doesn't matter."

I started to feel myself panic. "No matter how nice we are, there are going to be bullies. We can't stop them. We can't do anything about it."

I just wanted to go home and crawl in my bed. There was nothing I could do anymore. I wished my visions would just stop. I wasn't helping at all.

"Cat!" Becky said in a stern voice. "You listen to me. You are so right that we can't stop people from bullying. But..."

She stood up to her full 5' 3" height. "You're wrong, Cat. It does matter. We can make a difference. Remember on the bus when those kids were picking on me? You didn't give up, you defended me. You stayed my friend and encouraged me. You made a difference."

She looked at all three of us.

"We can be nice to others. We can still be there for each other. Right guys?"

Dallas added, "Yeah! We're in this together!

And off we went, with my heart still heavy, but knowing we would all be

there for Tim and Tyler. Everything
would turn out just fine.

Or would it?

CHAPTER 16

After a rough night's sleep, I slowly dragged myself out of bed for school. I had tossed and turned throughout the night. Tyler and Tim's visions kept playing over and over in my head. Becky was right, I could still be nice. I *could* make a difference. I wouldn't always have the right words to say. I wouldn't always be there to defend them, but, I would be nice to them. I would still be their friend.

Lunchtime finally came, after the morning seemed to crawl by at a snail's pace. Tyler had been quiet all morning.

As we sat and ate, I watched as my friends tried to lift his spirits.

After a little while, Becky and Dallas had to leave to finish up a project, and Grace had to head to class. So, it ended up being just Tyler and myself at the table.

"Hey, Tyler. You okay?"

He just looked at his food. "Yeah. I'm fine."

"I had a vision of the text Trent sent you."

I thought his eyes were going to bulge right out of their sockets. "You did?"

"Yeah, I did. I'm so sorry he sent that to you."

He shrugged his shoulders. "No big deal."

"Yes, it is. It was mean. So, so mean." I shook my head. "And it wasn't true."

"I'm used to it, Cat. I've been teased for my height and color forever," he said as he rolled his eyes. He looked down at his lap, "I just don't get it, though. It's not like I could pick the color or height that I am."

"I know. I think it's stupid."

We sat there lost in our own thoughts.

"You know what? I was just thinking back to when I was mean to others. I did it just to fit in. Holly would say mean things, and I didn't say anything, because I wanted my friends to like me." Pausing a second, "And, I think there are a lot of reasons people bully.

Some are jealous, some think they are better, and some feel threatened."

"Yeah, I wonder if some bullies get bullied at home from family and that's all they know."

"I've never thought about that. I bet you're right."

"I was talking with my mom a few weeks ago, and do you know what she said?"

"No, what?"

"She said people bully at all ages. The main reason is one thing."

"What's that?"

"Different."

"I remember you saying that when we were in the treehouse before. But, what do you mean, 'different'?"

"She said people fear things or others who are different than them."

"Hmm, your mom sounds pretty smart."

That got a smile out of Tyler.

"Yeah, she sure is."

"Well, lunch is almost over. Why don't we go find Tim and see how he's doing?"

"Okay. Sounds good."

As we stood up, I heard him say, "Hey, Cat?"

I turned to look at him, "What?"

"Thanks."

Now it was my turn to smile.

"No problem. Just do one thing for me, please."

"What's that?"

"Don't believe anything those guys say to you."

He held out his hand for me to shake.

"You've got a deal."

Then off we went in search of Tim.

We found him outside, standing against a tree. I could see he was trying to watch the group of kids play basketball but stay hidden at the same time.

Tyler and I slowly walked over to him. I didn't want to startle him and watch him stomp off. We walked up and stood next to him, not saying anything at all. We all just watched the game. I was trying to think of something to say when Tim surprised me and spoke first.

"Hey, Tyler. What did those jerks text you?"

I could tell it took Tyler by surprise too.

"Umm." He started to squirm a little.

"Don't worry. It couldn't be worse than what they sent me."

Tyler went on to tell Tim what Trent sent in his text.

I could see the anger in Tim's eyes. I always thought he looked down at his feet because he was so shy and kind of a weak person. I now realized he had just been struggling with his dad and some of the kids at school.

I had found that he would surprise me. Like when we were playing basketball outside for recess and he stood up to Trent. But at other times he would shrink back into his shell. It would be cool if others could see who he really was, when he was being himself and not worrying about being picked on.

If he just didn't have those lies being thrown at him all the time. It was so frustrating to see his visions. I just wanted to shake him and say, *they don't know what they're talking about! They're all lies! Don't listen to them!* But I couldn't do that. One reason being, I don't think I could reach his shoulders to give him a good shake.

"So, what did Trent text *you*?" Tyler nudged Tim.

That got me out of my daydreaming and back to reality.

He shrugged his shoulders and mumbled, "It was just stupid stuff."

"Come on," Tyler said. "I told you."

Tim looked at Tyler and his shoulders slumped, "Yeah, guess you got me there."

So, he went on to share his text.

I could feel my blood rising in frustration as Tim talked.

I blurted out, "I don't know why they say you'll end up like your dad. You're a different person."

"I know. I don't ever want to touch that stuff, because I never want to turn out like him."

"You won't," I said.

"You know what, Tim?" Tyler had been lost in thought for a while.

"What?"

"When my dad left my mom and me, kids were texting me saying I would do the same thing one day. And they said he left because he didn't love me." He took a deep breath, raised his shoulders and let them fall.

"Well, that's a stupid thing to say," Tim scowled.

"I know, but it's hard not to believe. My mom told me that my dad loved me very much. But she told me to always treat a lady how I would want to be treated."

"That's cool," Tim said. "My mom's been trying to get my dad some help. After the game, he lost it. He broke down crying when he realized they wouldn't let him in to watch my game."

Tim looked at us and continued, "He promised to go to an AA meeting."

Tyler and I just blinked at each other. We had no idea what he was talking about.

"What's an AA meeting?" I asked.

"My mom told me AA is a place that people who struggle with drinking can go and find help and support.

"Oh my gosh!" I squeaked out. "That's great."

"That's fantastic!" Tyler exclaimed.

"Yeah, well, we'll see if he goes."

"I hope he does. That would be wonderful," I said.

"We'll see," was all he replied.

The bell rang, and the three of us walked back together into the school.

All of us were lost in our own thoughts.

CHAPTER 17

As I was in the middle of my fifth hour class, I couldn't take it anymore. Holy cow, I must have drank my entire water bottle at lunch. I had to go to the bathroom so bad, I thought I might pee my pants. I quickly raised my hand and asked my teacher if I could be excused.

As I was in the bathroom washing my hands, feeling so much better, I looked over to see three other girls at the sink next to mine. They were fixing their hair and make-up. I kept quiet as I let the warm water run over my hands. They were talking loud enough for me to hear, and I recognized it for what it was: gossip.

"Oh my gosh, did you hear that Daren and Jenny broke up?" one of the girls exclaimed, pausing from applying her eyeshadow to glance at her friends' expressions.

"Yeah," a bored blond girl replied while looking in the mirror at herself, her lips tight against her teeth as she applied bright red lipstick. "I heard Daren dumped Jenny for Brooke."

"No way! I heard Jenny dumped Daren for Brian. Look." The darker skinned friend replied as she pulled out her cell phone, "Here's a picture of Jenny smiling with Brian."

"Well, did you see Daren's post? It said something about moving on to someone brighter and better."

"Oh my gosh, I think Daren is so much cuter than Brian. What was Jenny thinking?"

I rolled my eyes, because I couldn't take it anymore. I was getting so sick of rumors and gossip.

What good ever came from listening to it? Everyone's story was different. Most of them weren't true anyways. I had to get out of the bathroom before I lost it.

I quickly dried my hands and exited the bathroom, but as I rounded the corner, I almost slammed right into Mr. Williams's janitor cart.

"Sorry, Mr. Williams. I better watch where I'm going."

"No worries. How is your day going?" he asked.

"Okay," was all I could say. I was still so irritated by the girls in the bathroom.

"You know," Mr. Williams replied as he looked towards the bathroom, "you don't have to believe everything you hear."

So, he had heard the girls talking. I knew they were talking loudly, but I hadn't realized they could be heard from outside the bathroom.

I answered him, "I know, I'm learning that you can't always believe what you hear."

He opened his mouth to reply, but my two eyes connected with his one eye once again, I started to see stars...

It was years earlier when Mr. Williams was in middle school

himself. It was a football game and there were a group of kids standing off to the side of the concession stand.

"Guys, you will not believe what I heard."

"What, Kelly?"

"I heard that George Williams's dad beat him. That's why he looks like that."

"No way!" I heard kids respond.

"Yeah, can you imagine how much his parents must hate him? I mean, who could love someone that looks like him!"

"Yeah, I bet his own parents don't take pictures of him." The boy paused before continuing, "because he'd break the camera. He's so ugly!"

That got the whole group of kids laughing.

"Well, can you imagine your dad hating you so much that he does something like that? I'm so glad my parents aren't like that."

"Me too."

Just then another group of students were walking by and stopped to talk with them.

"Hey, what are you all laughing about?" A big kid that looked like he should be out on the football field himself asked.

"Oh," A girl answered, "You will never believe what we heard about George Williams ..."

As the groups turned and began to walk back to the stands laughing, a head slowly started to peer around the corner of the building. Right by where all the kids had been talking. The head inched a little farther around the corner until I could see the beginning of an eye. Then a little farther still until I could see... a patch. There was George. He had heard every single word those kids had said about him. Were they true? Not a bit. Did it make him cry? Maybe, but even worse...

It shattered his heart.

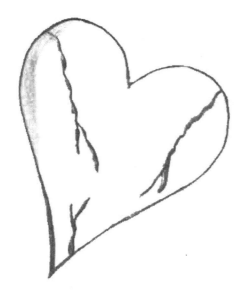

Wanting to cry myself, I just looked at him. I realized his lips were moving but I hadn't heard a word he had spoken.

"Sorry," shaking my head, "what did you say?"

"I said," he paused as the girls walked out of the bathroom and back to their classrooms. "I said, if you don't hear it from the person themselves, then it may not be true. Just be careful what you choose to believe."

I looked and saw a sadness in his one eye. As I turned to walk back to class, I heard him quietly say, "You never know how much you can break a person's heart by spreading rumors. Instead, look for a treasure."

A treasure. Now, what in the world did he mean by that?

CHAPTER 18

As I walked into school on Friday, I was greeted by my friends. They all started talking at once.

"What?" I asked, since I couldn't understand a word they were saying.

"Cat!" Dallas said. "We heard they're having an assembly later today and guess what the topic is?"

I shrugged my shoulders because I had no idea.

"Bullying," Tyler exclaimed.

"We always have speakers at our assemblies, what's the big deal?" I still couldn't figure out what was making them act so excited.

"I heard a girl say it's going to be someone famous!" Dallas exclaimed.

Becky got this dreamy look on her face, and clasped her hands together, "What if it's a movie star? A real-life movie star!"

We all looked at her, and Tyler leaned towards her, "Um Becky, are you okay? You're starting to scare me."

Becky snapped out of her fantasy and swatted Tyler on the arm, all the while grinning. "Oh, come on, Tyler, let a girl dream."

Looking at Tyler I asked, "Who do you think it will be?"

"I don't know. I'm kind of hoping it's a famous basketball player."

"Well," Dallas adjusted the straps on her backpack and started walking towards class, "I don't know who it will be, but they say it's someone really special, so I can't wait to find out."

"And, since it's on bullying," I said, "I just hope Holly and Trent are there listening to every single word."

Later that day, everyone filed into the gym. Becky and I were looking for Dallas and Tyler.

"There they are!" Becky yelled while pointing into the bleachers. "Oh, and Grace and Tim are with them. Come on, Cat."

So off we went to find our seats. Rumors had been going around like crazy today. Everyone had their guesses of who the guest speaker would be. I had even heard some say they thought it might be the President of the United States. As the gym filled up, our principal grabbed the microphone and tried to settle us all down. After everyone quieted, he went on to talk a little bit about being kind and not bullying. Then the moment came.

Our principal, Mr. Holman, stood there and announced, "And our very special speaker today is...."

CHAPTER 19

"Our very own janitor, Mr. Williams!"

The gym went so quiet, I could hear my heart beating inside of me. Everyone looked and watched as our One-Eyed, Scar Face janitor slowly walked towards the microphone.

Then it happened. I couldn't believe it. One by one I heard kids start to make "booing" noises. Most of the gym was now doing it, while also putting their thumbs upside down. I looked at my friends and they were all sitting there, wide-eyed with their mouths hanging open.

"Come on guys, help me out!"

I stood up and started clapping. My friends and Grace joined in.

"Yeah! Mr. Williams!" I heard Becky yelling.

We were drowned out by all the booing, but we kept it up until our principal grabbed the microphone back from Mr. Williams. He spoke loud enough and stern enough to get all of our attention.

"I cannot believe after what I just said about being kind, this is how you welcomed Mr. Williams."

A kid from the bleachers yelled out. "But they said it would be someone famous!"

"No! We said it would be someone special."

"Same thing!" A different boy yelled out.

"No, it's not."

I could tell Mr. Holman was getting very upset and frustrated.

"Listen, you kids are only in this school for a few years, then you will move on to high school. This man," pointing to Mr. Williams, "has been working here at our schools for over forty-five years. You have no idea how special he is to this community."

"But look at him! He's a *freak*!" A different student yelled out.

Just when I thought our principal was going to explode, Mr. Williams put his old gnarled hand on Mr. Holman's shoulder. He shook his head and whispered into our principal's ear.

Mr. Holman slowly handed the microphone back over to Mr. Williams and stepped away.

The gym again went quiet. Clearing his throat, Mr. Williams began speaking in his old shaky voice.

"I know I'm not anyone famous." He chuckled. "Not even close to a rock star, but I have something much greater than any famous person could have." He paused and looked around. "I have a love for this school. When I enter this building every day, I find myself so thankful to be here with you kids. My one eye is always watching. What do I watch for? I look for kids who are being kind, and I also watch for kids who are being picked on or bullied."

He was getting everyone's attention now. "The reason I can spot someone getting picked on or bullied is because I've been bullied since I was twelve years old,"—He pointed to his face—"when this happened."

I heard people gasp.

He chuckled, "And to answer a lot of rumors, no I am not a monster. I don't do anything on Halloween except lay a bowl of candy out on my front porch for kids to enjoy." He smiled, "I used to open the door and try to give the kids candy, but I scared them so badly that they would run off screaming before I could give it to them."

"Oh, how sad!" Becky's hand flew to her mouth.

I looked over and saw that her eyes were filled with tears.

"So, anyway, I am very pleased they asked me to speak today. I just wanted to share a story with you."

We watched as he pulled out what looked like a necklace from his pocket and held it up. "This was my wife's necklace. She loved pearls. I would buy them for her whenever I could. But I never knew why she liked them so much."

His eyes began to glaze over, as if trying to remember a distant memory. He stuffed them back into his pocket. "One day, she asked me, *'George, do you know why I love pearls so much?'*

*'*No,' I had answered.

'It's because they remind me of you,' she had said."

A few kids had chuckled at that. Mr. Williams put his hand up to quiet them. "I know what you're thinking, because I thought the same thing. I thought my wife was nuts. Had she just compared me, Mr. Scar Face, to those beautiful pearls she was wearing? I thought right then and there that I might need to take her to the doctor because I thought my wife had gone crazy."

That got a laugh out of all of us.

"She went on to explain what she had meant. She told me that a pearl is a treasure. When you see an oyster, it doesn't look pretty on the outside. But, if you take the time to carefully open it up, you may find a beautiful pearl inside."

He continued, "She told me that's what she found in me. She said that many people had spread a lot of false stories about me, but she chose not to listen to them. Instead, she ignored them and took the time to dig deeper, see past my outward appearance, and that is when she found... a treasure."

He paused, pulled out a hanky and wiped a tear away. "When I realized she didn't see my scars but saw me as a treasure, I didn't think my heart could love another more. So, from then on, I started to look for kids at this school who were picked on and see if I could help them. How could I help them? I tried to see past what they were being picked on for and treat them like a real person."

We could tell he was getting tired from standing. Luckily a teacher brought him a chair. He thanked her and sat down.

"Now kids, I need your help."

We all started looking around. How were we going to help him?

"These old tired bones can't work here much longer. So, after this semester is over, I'm going to have to retire."

"It's about time! You look like you're going to croak right there in that chair!" A boy yelled out from the bleachers and started laughing.

Before Mr. Williams could respond, kids all over the gym started yelling at the boy and telling him to knock it off. No one thought the boy was funny anymore.

I heard Tim yell out to Mr. Williams, "Sorry about that, sir, keep going. How can we help you?"

That made me want to give Tim a big hug. I was so proud of him.

Mr. Williams continued, "Well, thank you, son. What I need are students who will take my place. Not as a janitor," he chuckled and coughed," but I need kids who will stand up to bullying. I need kids who will be able to look past what they have heard about others. Not worrying if a person *looks* or *acts* different. I need kids who will take the time to slowly open that oyster and search deeper. Look for what is on the inside. Search for that pearl in others. What I need ..." he paused, and his eyes scanned the crowd, "... are Treasure Seekers."

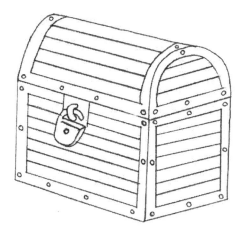

He leaned forward in his chair, "Who will take the time to seek for the treasure in others?"

Then the most amazing thing happened. The gym erupted as kids stood, clapping and cheering. I found myself on my feet joining in with everyone else.

After the gyms' echoes died down, and we all sat back down, Mr. Williams continued to talk. Well, he tried to. He was so amazed at the response of everyone that he got a little choked up on his next words.

"I want to ask you a question, then I will be done talking, and you can go back to your classrooms."

That got a lot of groans from the students.

"When you open an oyster, the treasure is a pearl. My question is..." He paused and looked around. "What is the treasure you receive when you look for it, and find it, in a person?" He slowly stood up and added, "Think about it and let me know what your answer is next week."

With hands shaking, he slowly handed the microphone back to our principal.

The next thing I knew, everyone was chanting "Treasure Seekers! Treasure Seekers!" I watched as Tim and Tyler started walking down the bleachers and joined Mr. Williams on the gym floor. They shook his hand, and both took an arm. They walked him out of the gym.

Which made the crowd go wild!

CHAPTER 20

That weekend we decided to have a treehouse meeting. We wanted to figure out the answer to Mr. Williams's question.

As we sat in a circle eating Grace's treats, we all just talked and laughed. I was so glad Tim had joined us. We were all having a great time getting to know him more. I think Tyler was super excited to not be so outnumbered by girls.

"Guys, it's all I've been thinking about the past couple of days," Dallas said. She put her hands on the sides of her head. "I can't get my brain to stop.

I couldn't fall asleep last night. I just kept lying there thinking of what the treasure could be."

"I know, me too," Grace said.

"Okay guys," I placed my fist in my open palm, "Let's think. He said he wants us to be treasure seekers."

"Yeah," Tyler bounced on his feet. "And if you are a treasure seeker, you are ignoring the things others say about that person and looking deeper."

"Hmm, to find a treasure," Tim said.

"Or maybe it's a prize!" Grace added.

"Oh! You could be right, Grace. Maybe we can look at it as a prize." Thinking, Becky continued, "But what kind of prize would a person get by being nice?"

"Maybe it's money." Tyler shrugged his shoulders.

"What? It wouldn't be money. You can't get that by being nice to someone."

"Well, let's see. If it can't be money, then what could it be?"

"Maybe it's cookies!" Grace passed her plate of goodies around again.

Looking at my sister and giving her a little swat on her arm, I smirked, "Well, if we were looking deeper into who *you* are, it would probably be food. But I don't think that's what Mr. Williams had in mind."

Letting out a big sigh, Grace took another bite of her cookie. With her mouth full and crumbs falling out as she spoke, she mumbled, "Then I just don't have a clue."

As soon as those words left Grace's mouth, we heard Tim's phone ding. We all looked his way. He leaned over and looked at his phone, his face turned red.

"What is it, Tim?" Tyler asked.

"Nothing." He pushed his phone away.

"Come on, you can tell us," Becky soothed.

He grabbed his phone and passed it to Becky. He grumbled, "Just stupid stuff."

We heard Becky's soft gasp, and she handed the phone back to Tim.

Looking at him, Becky quietly said, "Don't listen to him."

Now I was so confused. I had no idea what they were talking about. Tim then pulled his legs up to his chest and hugged his knees.

"It was just a text from Trent. It's no big deal."

"Yes, it is a big deal," I shifted nervously on the floor, leaning my head towards him, "What did it say?"

He handed the phone to me and I read out loud,

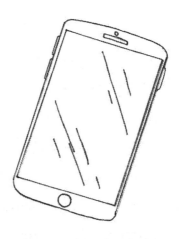

"TRENT: *Tim, you now think you are cool because you can throw a ball into a*

hoop. *Well, let me tell you, you're anything but. Look at your new friends. I don't know what they see in you. But come to think of it, I don't know what any of you see in each other. The school calls you guys the geek squad. Look at all of you. You have Dallas the Disease, Becky the Blow-Up, Tyler the Tiny, Cat the TRAITOR! and Timmy the Toothpick. Seriously, you are just a group of nobodies. I don't know how you all became friends. What a joke."*

Shaking my head, I handed Tim his phone back. I could feel the anger boiling up inside of me. I was just about to say something when Grace beat me to it.

"The nerve! How dare he!"

"Right, that wasn't nice at all!" Becky agreed.

"I know!" Grace hollered. I could see we were all upset about the text. Grace jumped up, placed her hands on her hips and stomped her foot, "He forgot ME!"

Everyone paused, we were confused for a minute. Dallas asked, "What do you mean?"

Grace's hands flew above her head, and her eyes sparked fire. "I *mean* he had a nickname for everyone here except me!"

We all burst out laughing. Instead of being upset about the names he called us, Grace was mad she had been left out.

"Oh my gosh, Grace! I love you!" I barked between bursts of laughter.

"Me too!" Dallas clutched her stomach in a fit of laughter.

"We may not be perfect, but boy, are we great friends!" Tyler said as tears rolled down his cheeks.

"Wait! I got it!" Becky yelled out. We tried to control our laughter, so we could listen to what she had to say.

"W-What?" My chest heaved, and my throat tightened, as I tryed to take a deep breath. Next to me, I heard someone start to hiccup, from a lack of breath. I couldn't help it, I started to giggle.

"I know the answer to Mr. Williams question! I KNOW what you get when you seek for a treasure in a person!"

"What is it?" We all said at the same time.

"It's..."

CHAPTER 21

Monday came, and we couldn't wait to find Mr. Williams. We just had to tell him our answer. After Becky had told us, it all made sense. We knew we had the right answer. Now, all we had to do was wait until lunchtime, so we could all go together and tell him.

As lunchtime *finally* arrived, we all met up at our table. I could see Becky was ready to explode, bobbing up and down on her toes.

"I'm just so excited! I hope no one else guessed it yet!"

"Let's go find out." I said.

We all started heading Mr. Williams'
way, but noticed a huge crowd was
standing around him. They were all
leaning in trying to give their ideas
first.

"Oh, shoot! How are we going to tell
him?" Dallas asked.

"I don't know." I heard Tyler say
behind me.

The closer we got, the more voices
we could make out.

"Is it money?" I heard someone yell.

Shaking his head, Mr. Williams just
smiled.

We heard a lot of people yelling out
their thoughts.

"Pearls!"

"Gold!"

"Food!"

Mr. Williams continued to shake his head back and forth. As the crowd slowly cleared out, we watched as people walked off with their shoulders slumped.

"I don't think anyone has figured it out yet," I whispered to Becky.

Grinning from ear to ear, Becky walked right up to Mr. Williams.

We all stood around and let Becky do the talking, since she was the one who figured it out.

"Well, hello, kids. How are you all doing today?"

"Great!" Becky replied, then quickly added, "We think we know the answer to your question."

"Okay, I'm all ears," he said.

Becky lifted her shoulders, leveled her eyes with his, and spoke with all the confidence that she had, "Your question was, *what is the treasure you receive when you look for it, and find it, in a person?* The answer is," She paused and put one arm around me, and the other around Grace, and answered, "*a friend.*"

A knowing smile formed on Mr. Williams face as tears fought their way from the back of his eye. "I knew you kids would be the ones to figure it out."

"How?" Dallas asked.

"I see you in the halls and at recess, always looking out for each other and never excluding anyone from being a part of your friend group. Like I said, I'm always watching, and I see you have found true friendship in each other. My work is complete. I can retire now, because you kids..." He looked at each one of us, "got it 100% right." I saw him smile the biggest smile he could with his scar.

We squealed in excitement and started giving each other high fives.

"Kids," his voice was raspy and urgent. We all stopped and looked at him.

"What?" I asked.

"How did you figure out the answer?"

"Easy," Becky answered. She turned and looked right at me. "Because we have lived it. We did have someone look deeper. She saw that there was more to us than what we were getting teased about."

"And because of that," Tyler grinned, "We're now all great friends."

"Yeah!" Grace and Dallas cheered, high fiving each other.

Tim quietly cleared his throat, demanding all the attention in the room, "Friends really are a special thing." He looked at all of us, "Not everyone has them." Dipping his head in embarrassment, "I didn't, until this crazy group wouldn't leave me alone and insisted on being my friend." He lifted his head up, and I noticed he had a smirk on his face, but I thought I could see some moisture forming in his eyes. "You guys really are great. Thanks for digging deeper to see something in me that I didn't even see in myself."

Right then and there, my crazy friends lost it. Grace, Dallas, and Becky were all hugging us and saying how much they loved us all. I knew we probably looked crazy, but you know what? I didn't care what others thought. This was a great group of friends. Crazy, but great.

CHAPTER 22

"Cat!" Grace hollered as she bounced onto my bed after school.

"What?" Looking up from working on my homework.

"Wasn't that the coolest! We figured out the answer!"

Smiling, I sighed, "Yeah, that's all I keep thinking about."

"Mr. Williams said we could take his place and become Treasure Seekers!"

"Yup, I know. Talk about awesome!"

"Grace!" I heard my mom yell from downstairs.

"Oops! I forgot. I came up to tell you that it's time for dinner." My sister scrunched her face, so her nose wrinkled, "And, mom and dad want to *'have a talk with us'*." She put her fingers up to make air quotation marks.

"Oh no, that doesn't sound good." My head began to spin thinking of the worst possible things that my parents could tell us.

"I know, that's what I thought. But mom had a little smile on her face, so I'm hoping it's good news."

But as I followed my sister down the stairs, I started to panic. For some reason I didn't think I would like what they had to tell us.

Grace stopped and turned to look at me. She saw me scowl. "Good grief, Cat, don't look so down. It could be great news." Her hands flew to her mouth in excitement, "What if they're going to have a baby? What if we get a little brother or sister? Oh, even better, TWINS!"

"Grace! Stop. Mom and dad are way too *old* to have more babies."

"Hey, I heard that!" My mom yelled from the kitchen. "For your information, we are *not* too old to have another baby."

Grace whipped around and looked at me, eyes as big as the bagel I had eaten for breakfast. She then went to hug my mom but stopped when she noticed my mom was shaking her head back and forth.

"Sorry, honey, but that's not the news we had for you. I am not going to have a baby."

"Awe," Our shoulders sagged as our excitement crumbled.

"Bummer," Grace murmured with her brows turned down.

"Come sit down. I made your favorite dinner, chicken and rice."

"I know, I can smell it," I took a deep breath, as the smells of spices tickled my nose.

"Let's enjoy our dinner and then we'll tell you the news." My dad grabbed his chair and sat down.

Groaning, Grace and I washed our hands and moved to our spots around the table. This was going to be a long dinner. We were just dying to know what they had to tell us.

Twenty *long* minutes later, as we were finishing up eating, my dad pushed his plate back and sighed.

Oh shoot, that was never a good sign. That usually meant it was something serious. I glanced over at Grace, and she looked a little worried herself.

"Girls, your mom and I have some news." He grinned. "We're going to move. We bought a house!"

"What?"

"We're moving! Isn't that so exciting?" my mom clasped her hands together in excitement.

"What do you mean we're moving? Like a different school?" I squeaked out. I felt like I might throw up my chicken and rice I had just eaten. And something told me it probably wouldn't taste nearly as good coming up as it did going down.

"I don't want to leave my friends!" Grace quickly stood up from her chair and gripped the edge of the table.

"Me neither! We have new friends, and they're great! We're supposed to look for pearls in others!"

"Yeah, we promised Mr. Williams that we would be Treasure Seekers! You can't do this to us!"

My parents look at each other with confusion on their faces.

"Kids," my dad started, "We have no idea what you are talking about. We don't have pearls for you, and I am totally clueless as to what a treasure seeker is, but-"

"It's someone who looks deeper than the outward appearance! You can't make us move! We were really excited about helping," I said with that panic feeling I would get sometimes. My heart felt like it was beating way too fast. My head was hot, and I felt like I couldn't get air. What if we had to move? What if we had to leave our friends? Who would search for the treasures in others? My mom must have seen the fear in my eyes because she started talking. Only, I couldn't hear what she was saying. I saw her lips moving but the sound wasn't going into my ears. Oh no! What if I passed out right here.

Maybe I would lose my whole dinner, right on the table in front of everyone!

"Girls," My mom piped in.

Okay. I could finally hear her a little bit.

"Before you go any farther and start panicking, let me just say, we are *not* moving schools, just houses."

It went dead quiet.

I heard Grace squeak out, "So, we're not going to a new school?"

"No, kids, same school, same friends. New house."

I let out a long breath. My heartbeat was starting to slow down. My head wasn't in a vice anymore, and I could hear what my mom and sister were saying. My dread of moving slowly but surely turned to excitement. But it quickly vanished. "Wait. What about our treehouse?"

"I can build you a new one, don't worry about that," my dad said.

"Okay," Grace added. "Tell us about this house then."

My parents exchanged looks and my mom said, "We can do better than that. Do you want to go look at it?"

"Yes!" We both exclaimed.

CHAPTER 23

After we helped my mom clean up the kitchen from dinner, we all hopped into my dad's truck. Before long we were on our way to our new house.

"Why didn't you tell us about this before?" I asked from the back seat.

"Well, it happened pretty fast," my dad answered. "We had just started talking about looking for a new house, and a friend, Bill, from work told me about this new development they are putting in. Bill and his family just purchased the house right next door to ours."

"Once your dad told me about it, we went and looked at it. We didn't want to get your hopes up if it didn't work out, but it did!"

"When will we be moving?" Grace asked.

"We can move in soon. The paperwork should be completed in a couple of weeks. And guess what?"

"What, Dad?" we both said.

"Bill has a boy about Cat's age. So, you might make a new friend. They will be new to the school district, so they won't know anyone."

"Oh, do they have any girls?" Grace asked.

"Yes, they have a younger girl. Maybe six or seven," my mom added.

Noticing we were driving for a while, I asked, "How far away is this house?"

"We're almost there. Just a few more minutes."

"Wait!" I sat up straight. Panic in my voice. "Will we have to *ride the bus*?"

Smiling, my mom answered, "Yes dear. But don't worry, it will be just fine."

"No! I don't want to move!" I yelled.

"What?" Dad asked. "Just because you have to ride the bus?"

"Dad, you have no idea how vicious the bus can be!"

"Cat, calm down. It'll be just fine."

Slouching back into my seat, I mumbled, "You have no idea."

Panic started to overtake me again. I could feel my chest tighten and my throat start to close up. Oh, my throat! I didn't think I could breathe! I started to roll down my window to get some fresh air.

"Cat! I'm freezing! Shut the window!" Grace snapped at me.

I heard my dad exclaim, "We're here, guys! Welcome to our new home."

"Wow!" Grace and I both said.

It was so new, that the grass hadn't grown in yet. The yard was still all dirt.

"Mom!" Grace exclaimed, sitting up straighter to see, "I love it!"

"But Grace," I choked out. "We have to ride the bus!"

She didn't even seem to hear me. She just grabbed the door handle and jumped out.

As I slowly got out of the car, I looked at what would be our new home. It was pretty. It was dark grey with white trim. But I liked our old house just fine. I looked around and didn't see any trees. How would our dad build us a treehouse, I wondered? Grace was grinning ear to ear, while I was struggling to take a breath.

Just then I heard someone holler to my dad.

"Oh, hi, Bill!" my dad yelled out and waved.

I turned and watched as a family stepped out of the house right next door to ours. They must have been the family from my dad's work he was telling us about. A little redheaded girl with pig tales stood right next to her mom, clinging to her leg. Next out of the house came a boy who looked around my age. With brown hair grown a little longer than most boys in eighth grade, he stood tall and just stared at us all. Turning, I continued to walk toward our new house when my dad motioned us to follow him.

"Come on kids, let me introduce you all."

I followed my family as they walked over to the neighbor's house.

"Girls, this is the man from work I was telling you about."

We started to make introductions, with everyone either shaking hands, or giving a shy smile.

I looked over to take a quick glance at the boy my age, Jonah. To my surprise he was looking straight at me. Before I could look away, our eyes connected. I faintly heard my dad exclaim, "Kids, meet your new neighbors," as I started to see stars...

If you enjoyed reading I AM A TREASURE SEEKER by Paula Range then watch for the next book in the Vision Series:

COMING SOON IN LATE FALL OF 2019:

Book #3 - I AM DIFFERENT by Paula Range

To find when the next book will be released please visit me on Facebook at:

www.facebook.com/paularangeauthor

I love to hear from my readers. Please send me an e-mail and let me know what you thought of the book!

paularangeauthor@gmail.com

Feel free to leave a review on Amazon to tell me what you think about Cat and her friends!

Books by Paula Range:

The Vision Series

#1 – I AM "NOT" A BULLY

#2 – I AM A TREASURE SEEKER

Coming later this fall:

#3 – I AM DIFFERENT

NOTE FROM THE AUTHOR

Rumors and gossip are everywhere.

If it is not coming from the person themselves, then it may not be true

You have a choice. To believe them or not. To spread them or not.

It takes a stronger person to not believe all the gossip, push it aside, and stand up for what is right.

Would you join me? Put the rumors aside, take the time to get to know others, and let's become TREASURE SEEKERS!

You never know, you might just end up with a new friend.

ABOUT THE AUTHOR

Paula Range lives in the Midwest with her husband, and five children. After being a stay at home mom for 18 years, she has started her love for writing children's books. When she isn't writing she goes on walks with her family or is busy driving them to events.

Illustration how to draw ideas from:

Art for Kids Hub
Stuart86

Made in the USA
Monee, IL
11 December 2019

18419507R00127